S0-BOE-647

If
the Shoe
Fits

Margaret K. McElderry Books
An imprint of Simon & Schuster Children's Publishing Division
1230 Avenue of the Americas
New York, NY 10020

Book design by Sonia Chaghatzbanian
The text of this book is set in Deepdene.
The illustrations are rendered in gouache.

Printed in Hong Kong
10 9 8 7 6 5 4 3 2

Library of Congress Cataloging-in-Publication Data
Whipple, Laura.
If the shoe fits : voices from Cinderella / by Laura Whipple ; with
illustrations by Laura Beingessner.
p. cm.
ISBN 0-689-84070-5
1. Cinderella (Legendary character)—Juvenile poetry. 2. Children's poetry,
American. [1. Characters in literature—Poetry. 2. American poetry.]
I. Beingessner, Laura, 1965- ill. II. Cinderella. English. III. Title.
PS3623.H55 I4 2002
811'.54—dc21
2001030778

To my mother, Ruth, who acted all the other parts
—L. W.

For my niece, Theodora
—L. B.

If the Shoe Fits

Voices from Cinderella

by
Laura Whipple

illustrations by
Laura Beingessner

MARGARET K. MCELDERRY BOOKS
NEW YORK LONDON TORONTO SYDNEY SINGAPORE

❧ Contents ❦

If the Shoe Fits

Cinderella's Prelude

Content with memories,
I am old and quiet now.
I remember the voices of my young life
like melodies on sheets of song
long stored in a dusty box.
I bring some out for you.

Many voices sang in my past,
each one precious, even my own.
'Twas a tale
of enchantment and spells,
of clocks ticking,
chiming bells,
glistening glass slippers,
and felicity found.

Gather round.
Listen . . .

Father's Ghost

Hear my voice first.
Blinded by a cunning woman,
I was the unfortunate fool
who set the stage
for the ashes and tears in this tale.

Left widowed
with a daughter,
my sweet Ella,
I remarried in a rush.
Rash move.
Reckless choice
for a new wife.

I planned to make amends
to my daughter,
but I fell from my horse.
A fast death.
No life. No remedy
then for my mistake.

What a fool to take
that woman into our lives;
a woman cruel,
uncaring at best.

I am only shadow now.
My poor Ella.
I cannot help her.
I cannot rest.

Stepmother's Rhythm

Ah, poor, poor, poor.
I hated the rhythm of
poor, poor, poor.
The poor seamstress,
expert, beautiful,
poor,
scratching at the world
for my own two girls,
for leftovers of aristocracy.
Poor.

I hated his wife's kindness,
even through illness,
her luxurious life
of leisure and jewels.
Hated her condescension,
as she bestowed on me
remnants of stiff lace
and green watered silk
to make dresses for
my own two girls.
With scraps, scraps, scraps.
I hated the rhythm of
scraps.

I waited and hid my pride,
covered my smoky anger deep
and feigned sympathy, concern.

Then she died.
He was lonely.
I flattered, demurred.
I was patient
and kind to his pampered daughter.
I let down my red hair.
I played a perfect part.
He surrendered.

He was not half as bold and strong
as I deserve, a woman like me.
I hated his weakness. I let him know.
I hated his joy with his daughter.
But I love the rhythm of wealth.
Ah, rich, rich, rich.
I love the rhythm of
rich!

Cinderella's Mourning

Father comes to my dreams,
though he is gone.
He is silent and sad.
"It's grief," Stepmother says.
"Stay inside.
Bare feet, coarse clothes
show mourning."
It seems right to dry
tears with sackcloth and ashes.

But we were happy,
Father and I.
Laughter we shared,
and music and song.
Dances, waltzes, mazurkas.
We danced long into evenings
around garden statues
and trailed strings to intrigue the stray cat.
I still feed our friend cat in the garden.

When mourning is over,
I'll honor Father with singing.
I'll sing to my new sisters
of castles and princes
and ships and magic.
We will sing
three-part harmony.

I'll honor Father with laughter.
I'll invent funny songs:
"The Rat Thinks He's Perfect, But Here Comes the Cat!"
I'll be Monsieur L'Air Dressier,
a marigold mustache mounted over my mouth,
and do up their hair in fanciful styles.
My two sisters will laugh
and they'll be my friends.

I'll honor Father with dancing.
We three sisters can waltz while we sing.
I'll teach them the mazurka
and there will be balls!
We'll go together, all of us,
and tell secrets later.

We'll ride barefoot on horses
through wet morning meadows,
and when we return,
we'll pick fresh garden herbs
for hearth-cooked omelettes.
We will eat together,
a family,
in the garden.

Thanks to you, Father,
I'm not alone.
You won't need
to be silent and sad.
I'll dream of your laughter
and your wonderful face
when mourning is over.

Garden Master

My garden.
Good my garden.
Cat is Master.
Cat is Cat.
In garden
Cat smells ratness,
finds swift birds,
slinks tall grass.

Good-Her gone shadow now.
Good-He gone shadow too.
Good-Young-Her
still pats,
feeds Garden Master,
smoothes me, Cat.

New Bad-Hers
kick me, Cat.
Bad-Hers chase me, Cat.
Hiss! Hiss! Hiss!
Scratch Bad-Hers
when Cat can.
Hiss Bad-Hers!
Hate Bad-Hers!

Clever Cat
mind-purrrrrrring
news of Bads
to Magic-Her.
Cat is clever.
Cat is sly.
Cat is Master.
Cat is spy.

Stepmother's New Rhythm

Ah, yes!—wealth.
Ah, yes!—power.
Ah, yes!—position.
The hour of comfort for
my own two girls.
My husband (dead fool!)
left his daughter to me,
an aristocrat, a beauty,
with her mother's kindness.
Nimble minded, intelligent.

But—
I have a new rhythm,
and a new rule:
She won't be smarter,
she won't be wittier,
she won't be wiser,
she won't be prettier than
my   own   two   girls.

She won't be seen!

None will compare
her features with theirs.
No.
In kitchen and stable
she'll be stowed away.
She'll prick noble fingers
with needles and thread.
I'll hide her inside,
sweeping cinders and dust.
Her mouth will taste nothing
but gruel and bread.

Slowly, like grapes in a press,
I'll crush this girl of
thoroughbred blood.

She'll be poor.
And shabby.
Dirty.
A drudge!

Ella of the Cinders,
"Cinder-ella,"
will never outshine
these daughters of mine.
Now is their time,
not hers,
by my command,
by my wish,
in MY house, for
MY   own   two   girls!

The King's Command

My crown has grown heavy.
My bones are uncomfortable.
Why are these courtiers
demanding my time?
Weary, I listen to
questions about everything,
questions of nonsense,
no reason or rhyme:

"What kind of feathers for the palace guard's hats?"
"Will flooding stop if we edge rivers with hay?"
"Should men's hair at court be long or short?"
"If we change all the clocks, will the sun obey?"

What folderol!
Time to retire.

Time to reflect, to study
in tomes and books.
Time to observe butterflies,
carefree and wild.

To be a scholar, a student,
not a judge and a ruler.
But then, where does that leave
my son, my child?

Now, my son, oh, my son,
is handsome, intelligent.
The heir to this throne,
the last of my line.
A good boy, but lately
mournful, moping,
morose, moody,
melancholy—
just grumpy
much of the time.

He must marry.
Become king.
Beget children.
Take over
affairs of state.
I'm tired, exhausted.
I quit! Resign!
Butterflies call,
butterflies wait!

I have a plan: (he'll hate it!)
I'll command a Grand Ball
where young maidens and men
will come flocking like sheep.

He'll despise the protocol,
pomp, and publicity,
but at least anger, not melancholy,
will sing him to sleep!

(And who knows whom he'll meet?)

Cinderella Alone

Who is this girl in the mirror?
The feet. Bare, dirty.
Where are her shoes?
The dress. Torn, dusty.
Has she no clean gowns?
The hair. Long, scraggly.
Where's a comb?
The face.
Tired tear trails.
The mouth.
No song.

I think it's me.
I see myself
and the trail behind me:
"Ella, don't be lazy.
You know so much about herbs,
please help with the meal."
"Of course."
"Oh, the horses love you;
please groom them for us."
"Yes, I love horses."
It seemed right to help;
we were family.

When they wanted more
and more
and more
and more,
I finally understood it was
too late for sisterhood.
It's a problem, a puzzlement,
what to do about me.
Just hoping is
an endless conundrum, a maze.
Father would say to me,
"Use your brain, my dear."

Something will come to me.
The garden's still sweet,
there are songs to sing.
No weeping.
No moping.
No melancholy.

I wish—I wish I were not—
not quite—
so alone.
Father . . . ? Mother . . . ?
I miss you.

Puss,
purr that you love me.
I'll sing you a song,
hold you soft in my arms,
and we'll dance in the garden.

The Stepsisters' Promise

Cinderella, stir those ashes.
Cinderella, tie my sashes.
Cinderella, you're always much too slow!

        Cinderella, place these laces.
        Cinderella, paint our faces.
        Tonight's the ball, but you'll stay home, you know.

Cinderella, fix my hair first.
Cinderella, stitch my gown's skirt.
Redo my hair the way I told you to.

        Cinderella, clean the stables.
        Cinderella, wash the tables.
        Polish spoons until they shine like new.

Cinderella, make our dinner.
Cinders Girl, why are you thinner?
The food we share with you is always free!

Cinderella, place these feathers
on my white cape made of leather.
I'm sure the prince is waiting just for me.

While we're dancing, sleep in ashes
and brush the soot from off your lashes.
Cinders Girl, why aren't you clean like us?

We'll tell you all about the waltzes
and mazurkas with His Majesty.
We promise.

What? Why are you crying?
Well, really, Cinders Girl,
don't make a fuss.

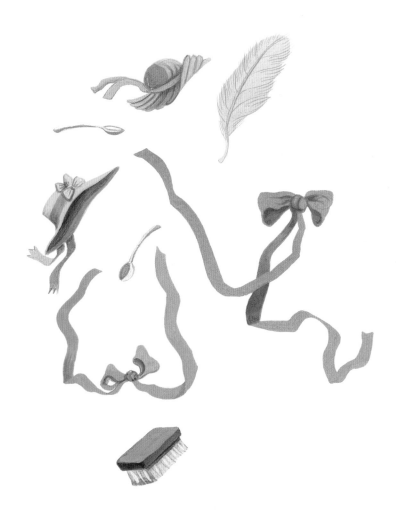

Cinders and Scraps

There is finally quiet in this dark house.
Cinders and ashes hiss in the kitchen fire.
The smell of white roses
floats through the door from the garden.
Small scraps of lace blow about,
abandoned.

My stepmother, stepsisters have gone to the ball
where they will have music and laughter
and dancing and light.

I had hoped it would be different tonight.

Can I waltz with cinders and scraps
and the smell of white roses?
Will there be laughter with garden statues?

Come to the kitchen, puss,
and sit on my lap.
We'll sit near the door
with cinders and scraps
and the smell of white roses.

Messenger Cat

Cat is messenger.
Cat is spy.
Cat is angel.
Cat is Cat.

Good-Young-Her
puts scraps out.
Feeds Cat.
Dances Cat.
Touches, pats.

Good-Young-Her holds Cat.
Says, "Sweet puss, dear friend.
I love you, Cat."

Cat licks salt tears—

Her's unhappy!

Must mind-purr news to—

Leap down!
That can wait.
Cat smells a rat.

Magic-Her

Someone is miserable,
someone's unhappy,
says my messenger,
says my spy.
Sent with a purring,
mind-melded melancholy,
from where is it coming?
Somewhere nearby.

Who is that weeping?
Aha! Poor young Ella.
What can I do
to make it all right?
She cradled my cat,
she's making my heart ache,
poor motherless child,
near the garden tonight.

Send a thousand gold pieces?
No, riches aren't happiness.
Send a plague on her family?
No, that would be cruel.
Send an army to rescue her?
No, I haven't the power.
Can she help herself?
Yes! She's nobody's fool!

But what?
Of course!
The core of Cat's message
gives me a clue—
the Grand Ball!
Send her!
That I can do!

She'll be like a princess,
dance partners in line.
Her fate and the prince's
might intertwine—
too improbable?
At the very least
she'll have a good time.

Garden Magic

So, get started.
Get organized.
Be efficient.
Need a checklist.
Think.
What's here in the garden
I can use?

Item 1—Coach:
Transportation for sure.
What for the coach?
A boulder?
Too heavy.
A peach?
Too light. (And sticky.)
A flower basket?
Too reedy.
A window box (dump the white roses)—
Zap!—will do.

Item 2—Noble steeds:
Horses from field mice?
Hard to catch.
The garden statues?
Too stiff and ugly.
Those brown lizards on the wall?
Zap! Zap! There's two.

Item 3—Driver:
A coachman, a coachman.
Cat smells a rat here,
a fine, fat rat.
A rustle in the rose bush—
Zap!   Zap!   Zap!
Zap!   Zap!   Zap!
(Stubborn rat.)

Item 4—Gown:
A beautiful ball gown,
as pearly as moonbeams,
elegant as waterfall
shimmer at night.
Shake the dirt
off the white rose petals,
add those few scraps of lace,
smooth them together,
spread on a trace
of cobweb designs
and silver starlight.

Item 5—Shoes:
What about feet?
She can't go barefoot,
dirty toes under the
dress showing through.
I know, sparkling raindrops
and my crystal ball.
Meld them together
for crystal, glass shoes.

That's all I need.
Ready for
Item 6—Ella.

Ella! Come into the garden!

Hunter Cat

Stealth—
Cat is stealth
in the garden.
Cat is hunger.
Cat is cruel.

Food—
Cat is hunter,
a machine who
smells ratness,
who needs fuel.

Machine—
mindless hunter.
Cat smells meat—
Cat sees rat!
Cat creeps.

Lights!
Flashes! Lights!
What was that?
Where is rat?

Sniff—
Ratness missing,
air smells clear.

Where was Cat?
Oh—

Stealth—
Cat is stealth,
in the garden.
Cat is hunger.
Cat is cruel. . . .

Blossoming

Who's in the garden?
How did this coach . . . ?
And horses . . . ?
Am I dreaming?
Where did this beautiful dress . . . ?
What are you, a new statue?
Mother?

Ella, don't close your eyes.
No, I'm not your mother.
No, I don't look like her.
I'm your . . . neighbor.
Your . . . godmother.
Oh, collywobble!
Never mind that.
Just pay attention, please.

You deserve some delight.
I can give these to you
for only one night.
Yes, dear girl, for the ball.

I can't believe it.
I can go to the ball?
May I wash my hair
and take a quick bath?
Where's my comb?

Never mind that. This is Magic.
When you put the dress on,
you'll be clean.
Don't gawk. Don't stall.
Move along.
You need to be seen at the ball.
Time's wasting.

Is it really true?
This dress soft as sea foam
and crystal shoes?
Oh, no! They're too big!

Never mind that.
Magic will fix them.
Zap! Zap!
Good.
You're beautiful.
Have a wonderful time.
Stop thanking me. Go!

No, wait!
Pay attention, please.
There's a small snag in my plan.
Watch out for midnight.
My enchantments lose power
as the hands of the clock
reach twelve.

Now go.
Claim each hour.

The Prince Grumbles

I'm shy,
but all females
(blast this ball!)
look at me.

I smile.
They slide past me
simpering so.

A bore.
Not one of them
gathered here
interests me.

I dance
with disgust as
lips whisper low:

"Good evening."
"I'm honored, sir."
"A fine ball."
"Yes, my prince,"

eyeing me
like marzipan on a
tray of sweets.

I dance
mechanically,
clock-watching.
Then I wince.

One of
these clods has trod
on my feet!

Wait!
Who's that?
Smile like moonbeams
on a splashing spring.

Who's she?
Tumbling dark hair
soft as milkweed floss.

Looks friendly!
Sparkling shoes tapping,
brown eyes snapping,
a laugh that sings.

My feet
stumble through the
thick hoards across

this endless ballroom.
"Excuse me. So
sorry! Beg pardon . . ."
In a trance,

I hurry and
hurtle, oops!
right onto her dress!

"Forgive me, my lady.
Would you allow me
one heart—ah—one darce—
ah—one dance?"

With a radiant smile,
she looks at her feet.
"Sir, my shoes say yes!"

She's clever!
Not boring
like others
who wearied me.
We glide
over the floor.

After one waltz,
"Is that all, sir?"
"No, my lady,
please more
and more
and more
and more."

Cinderella's Waltz

A waterfall of joy
floods me like enchanted dust!
I smile at a circle of spangled guests,
my father's friends.
They draw me in.
What Magic is this?
They don't remember me.
I do not tell them.

My stepsisters rush to welcome me.
My stepmother looks at me, confused.
Will the Magic protect me?
She says,
"Dear lady, we have not seen you
for many months.
Is your family quite well?"
I laugh and say,
"How kind of you to remember.
They are as well as you, madame."

My stepsisters say,
"Oh, my lady, come with us now,
join us dancing this mazurka,
we will show you all the newest steps.

"You must tell us who's your cobbler,
give us your dressmaker's address,
who did your hair—oh, my, here comes the prince!"

Then I see him bumping dancers
across the room, zigzagging
with some furious intent.
Toward us.
My feet tingle.
Are we meant to dance?

His rushing foot steps on my dress!
He asks forgiveness
and asks me to heart . . . ?
to darce . . . ?
to dance!

I laugh with him and . . .

I'm waltzing and waltzing,
his hand in mine,
I'm the Princess of Whirlabout!
Our hair intertwines.
Blurred colors surround us,
our eyes on the crowd,
whirling and flying,
laughing aloud.

Then . . .

Round two-three, sway two-three,
light on our feet,
barely skimming the floor
and our eyes chance to meet.
Lightning shards of crystal shoes
beat time with my heart.
This night's not the ending,
it's only the start!

Then . . .

Whirl two-three, swirl two-three,
out from the room,
circling and twirling
'neath dazzling moon.
Minute by minute
hour by hour
we waltz the time away
till the clock tower
rings the first bell of midnight . . .

deep,

tolling,

sad

hour.

Running

For the next three beats,
my heart is struck still.
Cruel ticking clock
ends our time at the ball.
Only seconds of joy left,
I run
through ballroom, hall,
out the door.

I run,
flying homeward
in light slippers of glass,
losing one,
bare foot sliding on grass
soaked with dew.
My dress? Shredded silver.
My coach? Smoky splinters.
Swift steeds and coachman
melt fast into small creatures
set free from enchantment.

I run
into darkness,
leave the slipper behind.
I call back into the night,
"Find my shoe!"
I have the mate.
I'll keep it forever.
A link?
Could it hold my fate?

Will he find me?
Who knew a girl named Ella
had been at the ball?

I run.
It's over . . . and all
I have to show for it is

this

one

shoe!

The Rat's Ride

Tonight I was scurrying by the stone wall,
nose sniffing, tail switching, all wary with worry.
The night seemed so strange, I
wondered if a cat had sneaked to the garden in search of
a meal.

I thought I heard bells.

I froze by the rosebush and listened with fear,
when a flash of bright light seared me. Then,
stretching and stretching, my muscles quite wretchedly
stretched and lengthened, took on a
new shape!

My useful front paws grew huge and became
heavy hands without claws, dangling down by my hips.
In place of hindquarters, long legs touched the ground.
I grew a flat face. Gone was my muzzle. I had
no snout!

Where were my whiskers, a-twitching, a-tremble?
This nose could sniff nothing of smells in the air.
Where was my soft fur? My sleek pelt, my pride?
My bare hide was covered with coarse cloth.
It scratched.

Where was my tail, long and slim, a-switching?
Totally gone! Just a memory of motion.
I tried to change back—shift—
shiver into rat shape.
Shrink.
Think rodent. Sniff for
ratness.

No luck;
I was stuck
in that clumsy,
big
body.

Then I was riding on a box with wheels.
It stopped for a long time
and now I sit, immobile, on top.
In plain view, where cats can see me!
I try to keep smelling for danger nearby.
Sniff. Sniff.
Finally, noises of running. Bells start
to chime.
Sniff. Sniff.
MORE enchantments this time?

I count bells—
nine, ten,
eleven, twelve.
Silence.

Sniff.
What dangers?
Sniff—Wait!

Something unique is
happening—*sniff*—
Oh, ratness!

Eeek, eeek!
Squeeeak, squeeeak squeeeak!

Free! Free!
I'm me!

Guest Gossip

Most annoying!
After she arrived,
the prince danced with
none of our daughters.

> Beauty can be deceiving.
> She's probably very common,
> maybe cheap
> under all that glowing, glossy,
> glimmering, glamorous—
> well, whatever she had
> is only skin deep.

> > Such a mysterious person
> > could be anyone, ANYONE
> > under that skin.
> > How did she get in?

I must admit she had an enchanting dress.
My wife needs to find that clever seamstress.

Disgraceful!
She monopolized the prince.

Our wits are dim!
We should have found someone
to rescue him.

And she left in a flurry at twelve.
Wasn't that rude?

What manners!
How crude!

Who said she might be aristocracy?
Royalty?

Who said they had been to
her family's estate for tea?

Why were they invited and not me?

What a mystery.
Most annoying!

The Prince's Regret

She's gone. We were dancing, light-footed,
as the clock chimed toward twelve.
I wanted to dance with her
on to the dawn.

Then she flew away, leaving me
standing there. She ran
across balcony and ballroom
downstairs to the lawn.

I followed her, shouting,
"Wait! Please wait! Who are you?"
She stopped by her coach.
"Find my shoe,"
her soft voice drifted back.
Her silver gown shimmered,
then faded to shadow,
and all of it vanished,
girl, dress, coach, coachman, horses,
in a flurry of smoke.
All gone, leaving small animals
scrabbling for cover
and me standing,
stunned, without hope.

Oh, I'm swift as a boulder!
Her name?
Don't know.
She should have told me—
I'm the prince!
No. No.
Must find her again.
How? When?

Slipped away like mist.
Wouldn't say her name.
Why?
Said . . . what? . . . Find her shoe?

Crossing the grass in dim light
from the ballroom, I see it,
luminous, her small glass shoe.
It's in my pocket.
An evening of happiness
is over . . . and all
I have to show for it is

this

one

shoe?

Second Thoughts

What have I done?

I was the one who cared she was crying,
who knew her distress.
I gave her a chance,
the fancy dress, the shoes—
my best work, the shoes—
two crystal shoes for her feet,
for music and dancing,
a regal coach,
a prince to meet.

And laughter.

But what about after?
Enchantments end.
Coach to wood fragments,
dress to rag scraps,
horses to lizards,
coachman to rat.
Poof!
All over.
That's that.

What has she now?
Only remembrance.
And she's still lonely.
She's no better off.

Of course!
All the Magic didn't end in shadow.
Marvelous!
Who knew the shoes would remain?
She has the slipper,
a shining secret
for memory's fingers.
He has the other.
Will the two shoes meet?
The end of this story
might be about feet!

Cinderella's Slipper

Hidden in her pocket,
my bright light shrouded,
I grieve for the glow of my mate.

Glittering hours
I remember, and music.
I was born for dancing
and the warmth of small feet.
So cold!
Oh! My shining is dulled.
So alone!
No step-together-step!

She touches me secretly
with fingers, not toes.
I want to kick her fingers!
How can she know
the pain of separation?

Why? I demand to know why!
When will she search for my mate?
When will we step together again?

The Prince's Quandary

Disconcerted.
Disillusioned.
Despairing, knocked
my head on the walls.
Distracted, I
forgot shoes, went barefoot,
shouting, "How? How?"
wandering the halls.

They sent healers and mages,
bags of possets and herbs.
Disgusted, disgruntled,
I waved them away.
Disquieted. Desperate.
A shoe wasn't her,
just a glass souvenir,
though I prized it each day.

Disorganized.
Muddled brain.
Thoughts sticky as glue.
One ball—
one night—
one girl—
one shoe—
the shoe!

Small, smooth, a crystal gem.
How many girls have
a foot so small?
Not many, I wagered.
I counted on it.
Disregard common sense,
and try it on ALL!

The Other Slipper

Abandoned
in the prime of my life!
Dropped!
Separated from my mate!

She-Who-Wore-Me
liked me well enough
while dancing.
Then she dropped me!

He-Who-Picked-Me-Up
cherished me at first.
Now, I, who was made for
small feet, must suffer.

Each day, a tougher trial.
Heavy, ugly, big feet
pushing down on my very sole!
Oh! I shuffle with pain!
Oh! I shudder silently!
The threat of shattering!
Oh! The strain on a shoe!

Why? I demand to know why!
When will he search for my mate?
When will we step together again?

Feet

Every day, I'm out here
trudging these streets.
Galumphing over cobblestones
in sun, rain, or sleet.
One small shoe and
two thousand feet!

Ugh!
Dirty feet and fat ones
with bunions like onions.
The big ones trying to fit
toes and heels into it.
Girls wheezing with effort,
the effort of squeezing!
The shoe straining to split.

A pox on these feet!
Tomorrow I'm giving up.
No one is enchanting enough
to compensate for this odious task.

Girls by the hundreds
want a crown on their head.
These two silly sisters—
can I stand these two more?
It's so tedious, boring.
Good, thank the gods!
Their feet are too big.
But—who's that?
Hair like dusty midnight,
peering out from the door?

The mother says, "Oh no, sir, not her, sir!
It's just Cinderella."
I say, "The shoe must be tried
on everyone. Let her come out.
In this house, we're not done."

She enters the room in tatters and rags.
Streams of hair ribbon across her brow.
Brown eyes shine in a smudge-covered face.
A small smile flickers over her mouth.

Could it be . . . ?
Her small bare feet—
tiny feet!—are coated
with cinders and dust.
I show her the shoe.
She says, "My feet say yes, sir.
Try the shoe if you must."

Those words!
It is she with that
half-mocking delight.
"Will you heart?" I begin.
She says, "You mean darce?"
I finish, "I mean dance."

My best partner
from that waltzing night
pulls out the other shoe!

Without enchantment
is she still enchanting?
She says, "I am Ella."
Her smile, a beacon like home
at a long journey's end,
clears all qualms.
Can I win her heart?
Will she be my princess,
my chosen, MY Ella?

The shoe fits her well.
Right, not tight, neat.
I thank the three women
and now I've found Ella,
I thank all those feet!

The Stepsisters' Reprise

Cinderella, oh, you sweetheart!
Oh, you darling, when do we start
coming to the court to visit you?

> Cinderella, do remember
> that you are a family member,
> what good sisters we have been to you!

Remember how we gave you pastries?
Pheasant with peach-brandied puree?
We even let YOU make them, goodness' sake!

> And I let you sew my best gowns,
> let YOU do my hair up stylish,
> let YOU try on my jewels and fancy capes.

Please, a regal invitation
to the palace habitation
of our sister dear would make me glad.

> I'd like to share food from your table,
> ride on horses from your stable.
> If I can't see your royal rooms, I'll be so sad.

We need to meet some handsome bachelors,
meet the king and queen and courtiers.
We've been kind to you, be kind to us.

> You wouldn't want to hurt our feelings,
> when we've been good and we're appealing
> to your sense of honor and of style.

Say yes, dear sister!
Oh! We're dying!

Well, really! Cinders Girl,
what's that strange smile?

Congratulations

Congratulations! Brava!
You freed yourself
from misery, cold cinders and soot.
With, I must admit, a little help from me,
a prince who was bold,
and an undersized foot!

Pay attention, please.
As I leave, I've four things to tell:
Item 1—remember the touch of rags and cold.
Item 2—recall the taste of hunger and ashes.
Item 3—share your bounty with others.
Item 4—use your own kind of magic
and you will live well.

Blessings

Good Cat,
Garden Master,
rumble-purring
good-bye blessings
on Good-Young-Her:

Good gardens.
Good meat.
Warm laps.
Good shoes for feet.

Good-bye blessings.
Purrrrrrr!
Purrrrrrr!

Cinderella's Doubt

It's all over, it's all finished,
soot and cinders, being barefoot.
No more rags and blisters; solitude.

Thanks, my puss, my prince, my father,
small feet, Magic, my godmother!
I'm overwhelmed with gratitude.

I will seek out those who hunger,
help those who shiver and are shoeless,
those with no Magic or good luck.

And my stepsisters, my stepmother?
They want to share my table, stables.
I must be generous, I have so much.

I'll invite them to my courtyard
for tea, strawberries, cheeses, pastries,
for conversation, music, and the arts.

Perhaps they'll even learn to love me,
for myself, not court and riches.
Perhaps.

Doubtful?

Perhaps not right now, but it's a start.

The Queen's Doubts

Who was she,
appearing like a sun shower on parched land?
She sparkled at the ball,
soaked our son's dry heart . . .
and ran.

Vanished.

He was mournful,
melancholy,
devastated, deranged.
And then . . .
that foolish foot-and-shoe thing!
And now, all is changed.
She has a ring,
a promise of marriage.

To our son.

She seems lovely, gracious, witty, bright.
Is that enough to make her the right
match for our son?
Her bloodline is noble,
but she lived like a drudge,
with pots and pans,
with buckets and brooms,
in rags, face smudged
with cinders.
What lies were hiding here?

Of course, we sent out spies.
And here's the truth:
Her father dead, three cruel women
hid her deep in her very own house,
a captive servant, the household slave,
with scraps to eat and straw for a bed,
but feathered luxury and red caviar
for stepsisters and stepmother.

The stepfamily's a problem.
A bond with these three
crude women is like eating sand.
Will she bring them to court?
Must I shake their hands?

I won't receive them.
I'll be occupied!
With needlework,
jigsaw puzzles,
playing the lute,
with plans to ride out in the town.
With painting and tapestries,
planning menus for balls,
with myriad fittings for gowns.

But—
what about Ella?
Does she like crossword puzzles and plays?
And music? And flowers?
Would she help gather white roses in evening hours?
We could have lunch in the garden with a daughter-in-law.
There'd be laughter, games, children playing tag round the trees.
Yes, babies, toddlers, grandchildren's toys.
Hubbub, feet running, small voices, and noise.

It's too quiet here.
There's a husband who loves butterflies more than me,
a moping son, morose, rarely carefree,
prune-faced courtiers afraid to smile,
dense gloomy silence all the while. . . .

Welcome, fair Ella!
To you I swear—
I will learn to love you.
You're an answer to prayer.

Father's Peace

Hear my voice last.
The tragedy
caused by my death
has passed.

I'm proud of my girl.
She's won
a prince to love her,
a king for a father,
a queen for a mother;
a real family
and not least,
freedom from my wife.

I'll leave this life
and become all shadow now.
I've found peace.

Cinderella's Coda

So, I was lucky.
I moved from good fortune
to hardship, to good fortune again
at that stage of my life.

Ah, you pause.
You ask three questions.
What about the rest of my life?
What would my life have been
without the Magic?
Did we live happily to the end?

I'll tell you only this:
The music of true Magic
sang only that once for me.
After, I had to compose
the music of my life.
Good luck in my youth
has allowed me to help others,
and I've had a share of great joys
and my own portion of sorrows.
I lost both my parents when I was young.
In old age I have lost my husband.
But I cherish both the joy and sorrow.
They complete my song, almost ended now.
I am tranquil.

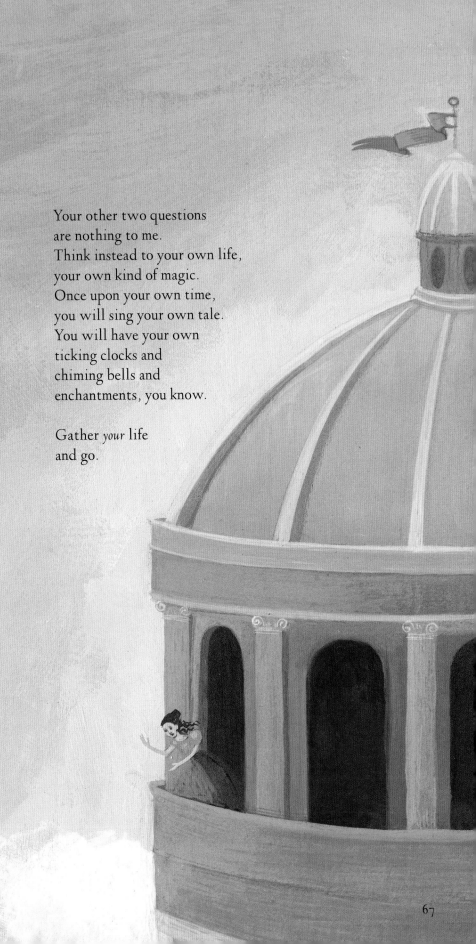

Your other two questions
are nothing to me.
Think instead to your own life,
your own kind of magic.
Once upon your own time,
you will sing your own tale.
You will have your own
ticking clocks and
chiming bells and
enchantments, you know.

Gather *your* life
and go.